A Glimpse Into Darkness

A Keepers' Chronicles short story

Michelle Birbeck

Published in 2015 by Michelle Birbeck
Copyright © Michelle Birbeck, the author as named on the book cover.

Second Edition

The author has asserted their moral right under the
Copyright, Designs and Patents Act, 1988, to be identified as the author of this work.

A CIP catalogue record for this title is available from the British Library.

Cover design © Michelle Birbeck
Cover photography © Eric Birbeck

Acknowledgements

Thank you to Alice and Phill, for joining me on this crazy ride, and being willing to read everything I throw at you.

A Glimpse Into Darkness

U.S.S.R., 1964

A phone rang somewhere in the house, breaking what little solitude I had managed to find. Small feet sounded as though they were pounding across the floor above me, each reflecting the painful beat of my heart.

I shook my head. Dwelling on what wasn't only made the pain worse, and no one needed to see me break down again. My attention was needed elsewhere, anyway. In front of me lay a pile of notifications that had found their way to the frozen winter landscape of Russia. Births, deaths, and marriages from all over the world were in need of inputting into the ever-growing records of my race. But now that my mind had drifted away from the monotony of my task, I couldn't help but be reminded of another time when I had stared at such a pile.

A quiet knock sounded, and I turned to see Lizzy, my niece, standing at the door. Her dark red hair hung almost down to her waist now, and it swung slightly as though she had just raced down the stairs.

"Shouldn't you be in bed?" I asked, forcing a smile to appear on my face.

"There's a man on the phone called U-Uf…" She paused and scrunched up her nose. "His name means wolf. He said you told him to call."

"Which phone?"

Lizzy dropped her head and shuffled from foot to foot. "The one in your room. But I knew it was going to ring, and mum is tired, and I didn't want it to wake her."

The slight look of fear on her face stopped me from reprimanding her for having been in my room. Was I so horrible to live with that my nine-year-old niece was afraid of doing something wrong?

The thought pained me.

I stood and wrapped my arms around her, lifting her up so she sat at my waist. "You did well, Lizzy. Now, shall we go speak to The Great Wolves?"

She nodded and grinned, and while I tried to reflect her good cheer, my own smile was a fraction of hers.

My phone call was brief: a few details, and a frantic Wolf. But those details were enough that I put Lizzy to bed and went to wake her grandmother.

"Helen," I whispered, shaking her shoulder gently. "Helen, I have to go out."

She blinked awake in the dark and reached up to rub her eyes. With a squint, Helen focused on me. Her hand searched through the dark for the lamp, and when she found it, the room flooded with light, making her cringe.

"Is everything all right?" Adrenaline opened her eyes wide and made her heart race. "Jayne? Lizzy?"

I placed a hand on her shoulder in an attempt to reassure her that her daughter and granddaughter were all right. "They're fine. The Wolves called. I have to go out."

She visibly relaxed with a drop of her shoulders and a sigh of relief. Then my words sank in and she reached out and took my hand.

"The vampires found them?"

I nodded.

"Be careful?"

"Always."

I left Helen in her room with a false promise to come back in one piece. The only reason I did so anymore was because I was all that remained. One last Keeper destined to wander the Earth fighting an ever-harder battle against a constantly growing tide of immortals.

It didn't matter that I was losing. How could one person possibly control the rest of the world? There used to be hundreds of us, all taking care of the delicate balance between the races. Now all that remained was me. With the vampires always vying for power and the rest of us trying to live in peace, clashes happened too often. And all too often I wasn't there in time to prevent the consequences.

Not this time.

When I slipped out into the freezing Russian night, determination pushed me forward through the wind and snow. Too many people had already died because I couldn't fight this war alone. I couldn't let the Wolves succumb to the whims of some overfed vampire.

Ulric, elder of the Wolves living in Russia, met me three miles from their hideout. Their home had already been destroyed once, burned to the ground while they slept. Now they were refugees, living in temporary accommodation until something more permanent could be found.

The elder's face was drawn and he paced a tight circle in the snow. Clenching hands showed how eager he was to shift from human to Wolf, but in my presence he would be stuck as he was.

"Ulric," I said, breaking his concentration.

"Serenity, you came!"

For a moment, the relief in his voice overwhelmed me.

No one should be that happy to see me.

"You said they found you?"

He nodded gravely. "One came an hour ago. Some of the young Wolves took chase, but I fear he was faster than we are."

"Is everyone awake?"

"Yes. They are packing now." He started in the direction of their latest home, breaking into a jog and then a run after a few feet.

I kept up easily, following the dark shadow of his back through the trees. Minutes later, we came upon their camp crudely thrown together from tents and whatever else had survived the fire.

Weres and their human partners raced back and forth, helping each other, gathering what they needed, discarding anything they didn't. No one looked up as we entered the large clearing.

Children sat huddled together, watching their parents with wide eyes. Snow blanketed them, turning dark hair white.

"I don't know what to do," Ulric whispered.

His gaze was fixed on the children. The sight of them, homeless and desperate, made my mind freeze as cold as the Earth beneath my feet for a moment. Ulric turned his eyes to me, and the strength of his despair proved enough to unthaw me.

"Head north," I told him. "As far north as you can get, and don't come back. I'll deal with the vampires. They won't follow you."

He glanced back at the children. "How will we know when it is safe?"

"I'll come find you."

Ulric's cold hand took mine, and he whispered, "We have stories of you. About your mate—"

Ray's name crashed through me, and I brought up a hand to silence Ulric whilst I composed myself. He stopped speaking and gave me the minute I needed. *No one* spoke of Ray. Not to me, and not to anyone else. Those who knew were all too aware of the effect the mere mention of him had on me.

My voice came out hoarse. "Unless you know where he is, I don't need to know."

No story, no matter how uplifting, could bring back what I had lost. Life was better when I didn't dwell on the past, on the love I once basked in, and the man I missed with everything I could ever be.

A Glimpse Into Darkness

Or listen to the tales people told of me.

Ulric smiled sadly. "Thank you, for helping us."

I nodded. "I'll find you again when it's safe. And I'll send your Wolves back."

Before Ulric could try to spin another tale, I took back my hand and offered him an attempt at a smile. The tracks of the vampire would still be fresh enough to follow, and if not, the Wolves left their own trails. Better that my mind focus on the task at hand than anything else.

Just outside of the clearing, I found the first signs that a vampire had been there. A single vampire, moving fast, heading, if I had to hazard a guess, right back to the rest of them. The direction was the same — back towards the burned out village of the Wolves.

My feet propelled me forwards, following the tracks as easily as if they had been painted red in the snow. Trees jumped out of the darkness, blocking my path for a moment, forcing me to dodge around them. Fallen branches threatened to trip me, and snowdrifts filled the clearings.

As the first light of a grey day filtered down through the canopy, I slowed. The harsh smell of the still smouldering village assaulted my nose. Snapping jaws and thuds filled the early morning.

I came to a halt barely fifty meters from the village wall. A brisk wind told me everything I needed to know. Three Wolves. One vampire. Twenty buildings fit only for nature to reclaim them.

The wind shifted, blowing in from the east. Two more vampires, moving slowly. The scent of them filled my nose, but no sound of them travelled with the breeze. Perhaps they had stopped, as I had, and were biding their time before helping their cornered accomplice.

Three on three were too even to be good odds for young Wolves.

Cautiously, I eased closer to the village until I had a clear view of the Wolves. They had the vampire encircled, wagging their tales as they snapped at him. Almost playfully, they took it in turns to lunge, coming within inches of the vampire's flesh.

Towering in the middle, the male vampire grinned. His arms hung at his side, as though the sight of three Wolves was as harmless as yelping puppies.

But even young Wolves were imposing; all snarling faces, clawed paws, and fur that rippled with the strength hidden beneath. Few stood calmly when Wolves circled.

The faintest crunch of a breaking twig drew my attention. The other vampires were moving; slowly, but moving.

Time the children went home.

As I went to step out into the ruined village, something stopped me. A thought. If I sent them running now, the other vampires could follow, and everyone would be in danger because of my eagerness to solve the problem.

With a faint sigh, I stayed where I was, reduced to watching as the Wolves played.

Frustration wormed its way through me as I waited, almost making me fidget. As the years had passed, a darkness had taken root in me. It made me eager for the fight, impatient for the moment when I got to live up to my alter ego.

It filled me now with a perverse kind of joy. Nothing compared to the happiness that had once driven me, but a joy nonetheless.

Moments later, as I dwelled on memories that made my heart clench, two vampires walked into the village.

Sadistic grins spread across their faces when they spotted the three Wolves.

It would have been easy to influence all three of the vampires to turn around and never return. Enter their minds, change what they thought, and alter their reasoning for being here. One mistake, however, and they would come back.

Out I stepped into the village. A loud crack of stone as it shifted under my feet drew all eyes to me.

"Time to go home, kids," I called. "I'll take it from here."

They hesitated, unsure what to make of me. All it took was a mention of their elder and they raced off into the trees. Home was where they needed to be. Away from what was coming.

The vampire who had been surrounded sauntered across what was once a street to join his friends. "We can track them."

A Glimpse Into Darkness

"Not when I'm finished with you."

"Oh? And what's a pretty little thing like you going to do to us?" He flashed a set of fangs that should have been intimidating.

I smiled in return and shrugged. "Why don't we find out?"

Three on one were odds I liked, for me.

Each of the vampires charged forward, expecting something easy to kill, I was sure. Maybe they thought I was another Wolf come to rescue the children. They soon knew otherwise as I easily evaded their attacks.

First one grabbed at my throat, only to find himself howling in pain as I snapped his forearm. The second took a different approach, aiming low. He came at me making one mistake: he took his eyes off me.

No sooner had he looked away than my fist came down, complete with dagger, on the back of his neck. He fell flat with a dull thud in the snow.

One left that wasn't injured and he had seen all my moves or so he thought by the way he slowed to a crawl. I grinned as he circled me, waiting for an opening. He had learned quickly that any kind of head on attack would end with incapacitation. Shame.

Snow began to fall as we circled in the ruined street. It fluttered down in a slow procession that would soon obliterate everything here. By the time night fell, there would be no trace of today's events. The smouldering village would be left to ruin, and the Wolves would never return.

So long as I dealt with the vampires here and ensured no others would follow.

Cautious as the vampire was, ever circling, he still underestimated me. I allowed no trace of my movements to give me away before I lunged. An arm around his waist. A fall into fresh snow. A brief struggle in the wet before the snap of bone left his body limp.

Blank eyes stared up at me. He wasn't dead, not yet. Most vampires could heal a broken neck given enough time. And here, deep in the overcast state of winter, the sun could not reach him to burn the remains.

I dragged a second bone dagger from my boot, and took my time in using it. These days the fact that I might be preventing the crossing over of a vampire by not burning this last piece of him didn't bother me as much as it should.

Sharp bone slid easily into the vampire's chest. The blade cut through his heart, killing him. No vampire could survive a dagger made from the bones of their own. Not through the heart.

Deed done, I rose and turned my attention to the other two. Another with a snapped neck, still alive if he had enough power. And one with a broken arm, crawling away in pain.

He would wait. I had questions for that one.

Same dagger, different chest, and the second of the three lay dead, waiting to be dismembered and burned.

The last still crawled, hugging his broken arm. He couldn't have been more than half a century old. Too young to know that all pains fade, and yet too old to let Wolves faze him.

I approached him slowly, letting him crawl farther towards the relative safety of the forests. His whimpers seemed loud in the quiet of the falling snow. Out of place, almost, in the idyllic setting of a razed village partially covered in ice.

I stepped on the vampire's trailing foot, bringing him to a shuddering halt. He was young enough to be scared at least.

When he huddled into the snow, as though he could disappear and I would leave him alone, I flipped him to his back and knelt on his chest.

"How many others know?" I asked sweetly. Better to give him a chance to tell me.

The only response I got was a whimper.

"Come now, I can make this quick if you just tell me."

I offered him a smile and eased off his chest a little, attempting to lull him into a sense of security.

"You'll let me go?" he asked.

"Maybe." To the other side of life at least.

Of course, I could retrieve the information for myself. A simple task of entering the vampire's mind, searching out what I wanted, and making him forget he ever knew. But there were times, more so of late, when looking into the minds of these power hungry creatures stirred something in me. A thing much darker than the desire to smile whilst I killed them. A thing I had a name for, but one I dared not utter for fear I would act upon it.

Times like those, I had to remind myself that slaughtering them all was not the way forward. Killing every vampire on the planet would make me as bad as them, and I *refused* to become them.

"Will you tell me?" I asked again.

Still the vampire stared at me with wide eyes and closed lips.

Silence filled the void but could not provide the answer I wanted.

"If you won't tell me, I will make you."

A flash of the dagger in my hand had the vampire trembling. His whimper beat back the silence but for a moment before it turned into a pleading scream that shattered it.

"No! No! I'll tell you!"

I leaned in close. "Then tell me, before I grow bored."

His eyes grew impossibly wider, and he struggled to stutter out his answer.

Rising from his chest, I huffed in frustration. Some of them were so damned stubborn. Perhaps he needed motivating.

I threw the dagger, landing it perfectly in the vampire's thigh. He howled in pain as the blade sliced through his flesh. Blood, thick and cold, welled around the knife as it shifted with his cries.

He muttered something that was obscured with his pain, and I knelt by his side, hoping to hear better.

"No one!" he said again.

To be sure, I took hold of the knife and twisted. "Who else knew?"

"No one! No one! I swear! No one!" And this time I was inclined to believe him, though I still checked his mind to be sure.

With a yank, I pulled the dagger free. "Thank you."

When I brought it up to his chest, he stared at me and whispered, "Who *are* you?"

The grin I gave him was as dark as my answer. "I'm Azrael."

Dark had begun to fall by the time I had dismembered the three bodies and started the fire. Each piece burned with a faint purple edge and reeked of death. By the time the last head had been placed in the flames, my body was warm and my clothes and hair stank of vampire.

Still, the job had been done, and the Wolves were now safe. Not safe enough to ever return to their home, but enough that they could live in peace in a new one.

I watched the flames make the night bright until the darkness won against them. When the fire died, I started north, back towards where the Wolves had been last.

As I raced through the dark, I thought I should feel some guilt for what I had done. Some pang of hatred towards myself for inflicting such pain on another to get my way. But all I felt was as cold as the snow around me. The world may as well have been in black and white for all the colour meant to me, with a temperature that barely rose above freezing.

At least the cold left me numb to all the things I didn't want to remember. It let my mind switch off for a while and stop wondering, searching, and most hurtful of all, hoping.

Hope should have died years ago, but instead it reared its head from time to time, as if the world wanted my agony to stay fresh in my mind. No help needed with that. Not when every breath I took and the very beats of my heart did that job well enough.

Before my mind could wake from its frozen state and burn me alive, a growl cut through the air. Up ahead stood a Wolf, dark in the night but streaked with pale markings that I didn't recognise. Its scent gave away that it was a Were, but it wasn't one of the three young ones I had sent home.

"Easy," I whispered, coming to a full stop and holding my hand out in front of me. "I'm here to help."

Yet the growing continued.

"You'll need to move away if you want to shift back to human…"

Instead, the Wolf charged, springing forward as if to attack. Too late I remembered that I stank of vampire, and any Wolf who didn't recognise me would think me a threat.

The animal fell upon me with snapping teeth and raking claws. I blocked as best I could, but without hurting the Wolf my options were limited.

A claw caught my cheek, tearing into my skin with a blazing agony. Teeth clamped down on my shoulder and shook me. Pain lanced through me, forcing me to let go. No sooner had I dropped my arms, than the Wolf switched its grip and went for my throat, teeth piecing my flesh with practiced ease.

The last thing I remembered before I passed out was Ray. A name. A face. And a deep regret that I hadn't found him. If only to say goodbye.

That I was able to open my eyes and was still alive came as a mixed blessing. Selfishly it irked me that death hadn't come, even though I knew what it would take before that could happen. The rest of me, however, realised that as life still flowed through me, it meant I could protect the world for a little longer yet.

Tentatively, I turned to my side. Nothing pulled or ached when I did, so I risked sitting up. Tenting rippled around me, blown by a gentle wind. Light streamed in, amplified and warm inside the tent.

When I glanced down at myself, I found I was in different, blood free clothes. Gone were my dark jeans and top, replaced by ill-fitting men's trousers and a loose shirt. They were clean, and I no longer smelled as though I had been burning vampires all day.

Voices drifted on the soft breeze. Happy voices.

The Wolves. It could only be them who had cleaned and changed me.

My boots stood in the corner of the tent, and I tugged them on before unzipping the door and stepping out into the sun and snow.

Everything around me came to a sudden halt. The voices ceased. People stopped talking and stared. All the attention made me want to crawl back into the tent for a while.

Ulric saved me. He bounded across the snow with such a smile on his face. I thought for a moment that he might fling his arms around me, but he stopped a couple of feet short.

"You are alive!"

"Very hard to make me otherwise." My words sounded happier about that than I felt.

"I have someone who needs to apologise to you." He turned away and beckoned to someone I couldn't see.

The young man who approached shuffled through the snow, head down, hands fidgeting. He finally looked up when he got to Ulric's side, and straight away I saw the family resemblance. Same dark eyes, wide set and open. Mirrored jaws with sharp lines and nearly pointed chins.

"This is Ulric, my son."

"Doesn't that get confusing?" The question came out before I could stop it.

Ulric laughed, but his son did not. "Sometimes. Especially when we are in trouble."

The son smiled. "We never know which one of us mum is shouting at."

"Or what she is shouting for this time."

The pair looked at each other and shared a moment. When Ulric nudged his son, he turned to me, with such a serious expression on his face that I knew why he needed to apologise.

I put my hand up to stop him. "No need," I said with a shake of my head. "You didn't know who I was, and I realised far too late what I must look like."

"Still, you almost died, and that is my fault."

I shook my head. "It was no one's fault, and I'm fine."

"If there is anything I can ever do to repay you, please, I would like to."

No doubt Ulric had already begun grooming his son to take over as elder one day. I could see it in his stance and determination, and hear it in his words.

"There is one thing you could do," I said, an idea forming.

A Glimpse Into Darkness

"Name it."

"Let me help you rebuild. I have contacts, friends, people who can be trusted. There may only be me left, but my race is spread far and wide. Let me help you and that will be repayment enough."

He gave me the strangest look through narrowed eyes, and then opened his mouth as if to speak, but nothing came out. Twice he tried, and twice all he got out was an unintelligible sound.

Eventually he managed, "Why would you do that for us?"

All I could do was shrug. "Because I'm a Keeper. It's what we do. We help. We keep the balance. We're here to make sure no one race takes too much power. What those vampires were doing, it wasn't right. To have burned down your homes and tried to kill you…" I paused and shook my head. "It shouldn't have gotten so far."

Ulric, the father, spoke up, "You speak as in the old days, the ones my grand father spoke of. When you were many and the world seemed at peace."

"Sorry." I turned away from them to hide the pain I felt.

I hadn't realised I had been saying "we." It should have been I. "We" were no more.

A warm hand squeezed my shoulder. "Thank you for the offer, Serenity. We would be honoured to accept."

Three hours, several offers of food and thanks, and some planning later, I managed to excuse myself from the rejoicing Weres. With their homes gone and their lives upheaved, it seemed strange to see them dancing and laughing. But they were safe, and their new homes would be ready soon enough. Nestled against the edge of a ravine, they had steep cliffs for protection, running water flowing freely down into it, and enough shelter from the weather on all sides to see them comfortable.

I made my excuses and headed back home. Russia may have been frozen, but its sparsely populated lands made the journey pass quickly. Soon enough, however, I had to slow for traffic and people. I kept my head down and my pace quick but acceptable.

By the time I saw my house, I had influenced half a dozen people from asking me if I was all right. A woman wandering the streets without a coat was a sight indeed in the winter. Most thought I was mad.

I barely got to my front door before it swung open and little Lizzy bounded down the steps and flung herself into my arms.

"Aunt Sere!" she cried, clinging to my neck. "Can I meet them? Please?"

Her eagerness drew a rare laugh from me. "Maybe when you're older."

"Aww!"

"Sweetie, the Wolves can be dangerous…"

"I know." She frowned and hugged me tight for a moment. "I didn't like seeing you sleeping."

As she held me, I carried her into the house, and found Jayne and Helen waiting in the living room. Dark circles decorated Jayne's eyes again, and I wondered if it had been Lizzy's gift of second sight or memories of her husband that had kept her awake this time.

Helen spied me before I could announce my arrival, putting a stop to any questions I almost asked.

"Sleep well?"

"How long have I been gone?" I hadn't thought to ask the Wolves.

"Six days."

That meant I had been unconscious for around three. "Sorry."

"No you're not."

I passed Lizzy over to her grandmother, and took a seat opposite the three of them. "The Wolves are safe. That's all that mattered."

Helen placed her hands over Lizzy's ears and dropped her voice. "And the fact that this one woke up screaming in the middle of the night?"

"Is she all right?" I whispered.

"She'll be fine. You always come back."

"And I always will."

Helen glared at me. Jayne shook her head and turned away again.

A Glimpse Into Darkness

"I am sorry," I told them. "The Wolf didn't recognise me. I didn't intend to get mauled."

Jayne rose and patted my knee as she passed me. "You never do, Aunt Sere. You never do."

I waited until I heard Jayne shut her bedroom door until I spoke again. "Is she very mad at me?"

Helen shook her head. "No. She's just tired, Serenity. We all are."

She didn't let me apologise again, instead she removed her hands from Lizzy's ears and smiled widely. "Pancakes for dinner?"

Lizzy nodded excitedly, her hair bobbing up and down with her.

"Go on then, go get the ingredients out."

She raced out of the room, having clearly forgotten ever being scared or woken in the night by her dreams. I envied her that.

Helen rose slowly. She stopped in front of me and stared down. "You *will* join us for dinner tonight."

She raised a hand and cut off my protest. "I don't want to hear it, Serenity. Go shower and change, and drag that daughter of mine downstairs. We could all do with a family dinner tonight."

I watched her walk out of the room, and only when she disappeared did I let myself sink into the chair and run a hand over my face. It took me a moment to be able to move again.

For everyone else, I reminded myself. I wasn't doing any of this for me anymore. Everything I did was either for the good of the races or for the good of my family. What I wanted I couldn't have. Everyone else was the next best thing.

The Last Keeper

The Keepers' Chronicles Book 1

Did you ever wonder what's stopping the vampires from taking over?

The Keepers have the power to influence the mind, keeping the immortal races of the world hiding in the shadows. Betrayed by their own centuries before, they've been hunted to near extinction and slaughtered at every opportunity.

Two are all that remain, all that stand between the immortals, the human race, and total destruction.

Serenity Cardea is the only one left impervious to death. But with her last brother living a mortal life with his weakness at his side, Serenity is left alone to uncover who betrayed their secrets and find a way back from the brink of extinction.

On her own, Serenity is indestructible… but all that changes when she meets Ray Synclair.

Now her days are numbered, and any one could be her last…

Last Chance

The Keepers' Chronicles Book 2

With her race saved from extinction, Serenity's life could not be better. Married, finally, to history professor, Ray, and back in London for the first time in a century, retirement isn't coming easy. Being a housewife was never in her make up.

But when Lizzy calls to say the Keepers' records have been taken, retirement is preferable over the danger they now face. All their family trees. Historical and current details of every Keeper across the entire globe... gone... stolen.

Targets once more, Serenity's isn't inclined to sit back and let her brothers and sisters face the losses she witnessed. The order to move the Keepers' entire race seems their only option, but it comes at a price. One that all too soon becomes clear.

Whoever is behind the threat, they show no remorse for their actions and no compassion. Entire families are decimated, leaving no one alive. Serenity can only be pushed so far before she breaks, and when the threat starts taking the lives of the race's children, enough is enough.

No matter who is behind the threat, they will not face the endless mercy the Keepers have always displayed.

No matter who is responsible for the killings, no threats will be issued.

No matter if the killers are human, witches, Weres, vampires or even Keepers... This time, there will be no survivors.

Exposure

The Keepers' Chronicles Book 3

The Seats are long dead. And after more than two centuries, the vampire world is stable enough for Serenity to settle down into a quiet, happy life.

Until July 4th on the celebration of Independence Day. Centenary celebrations in Times Square broadcast the world over.

It should have been a joyous occasion, another in the long line of human milestones Serenity and her vampire family have witnessed. That is until a vampire chases a woman into the crowd and drains her dry on the summer's day.

With the news of vampires spreading quickly across the globe, Serenity must stand up and tell the human race that they are not alone in the world. And when they react with force instead of open arms, she must lead the Keepers in the biggest decision her race has had to make.

From keeping the vampires in the shadows to being their protectors, the Keepers, and Serenity most of all, face the fight of their lives to keep the human race from slaughtering all vampires on sight. But with a war between the races on the line, one mistake can mean the difference between keeping everything Serenity has ever worked for and burning the world down around her.

Revelations

The Keepers' Chronicles Book 4

No one knows where the Keepers came from. Not even Lizzy Walters, who has the ability to see both the past and the future. In fact, there is only one thing Lizzy can't see, and that is the dead. Yet her dreams for more than a hundred years have involved impossible futures with impossible consequences.

But all thoughts of the dead are soon swept aside when a mysterious plague takes hold of the Weres. Their shifts are killing them, turning the flowing of forms into a death sentence of broken bones and torn bodies.

There is only one person alive capable of saving the Weres, but Georgianna Rose, Crone to all witches, hasn't been seen in centuries.

Lizzy must race against death to find a witch who doesn't want to be found, and in the process uncovers truths about the world she may wish had stayed buried.

Books by Michelle Birbeck

The Keepers' Chronicles

Other Novels

Short Stories

About the author

Michelle has been reading and writing her whole life. Her earliest memory of books was when she was five and decided to try and teach her fish how to read, by putting her Beatrix Potter books *in* the fish tank with them. Since then her love of books has grown, and now she is writing her own and looking forward to seeing them on her shelves, though they won't be going anywhere near the fish tank.

You can find more information on twitter, facebook, and her website:

Facebook.com/MichelleBirbeck
Twitter: @michellebirbeck
www.michellebirbeck.co.uk